5-Minute Amelia Bedelia Stories

by Herman Parish ❀ pictures by Lynne Avril

Greenwillow Books, *An Imprint of* HarperCollins*Publishers*

Gouache and black pencil were used to prepare the full-color art.
Amelia Bedelia is a registered trademark of Peppermint Partners LLC.

Amelia Bedelia 5-Minute Stories
Text copyright © 2020 by Herman S. Parish III
Illustrations copyright © 2011, 2012, 2013, 2014, 2015, 2016, 2017, 2018, 2019 by Lynne Avril
Based on Amelia Bedelia books written by Herman Parish and illustrated by Lynne Avril.
 Manufactured in China. For information address HarperCollins Children's Books,
a division of HarperCollins Publishers, 195 Broadway, New York, NY 10007.
www.harpercollinschildrens.com

Library of Congress Control Number: 2019948737

ISBN 978-0-06-296195-2 (hardback)

20 21 SCP 10 9 8 7 6 5 4 3

First Edition

Greenwillow Books

•Contents•

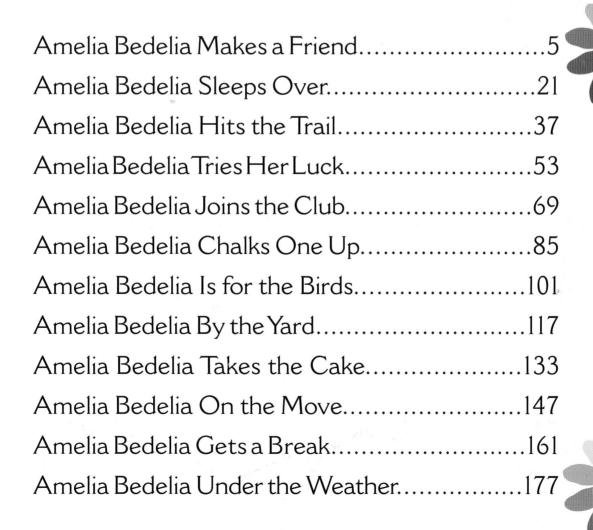

Amelia Bedelia
·Makes a Friend·

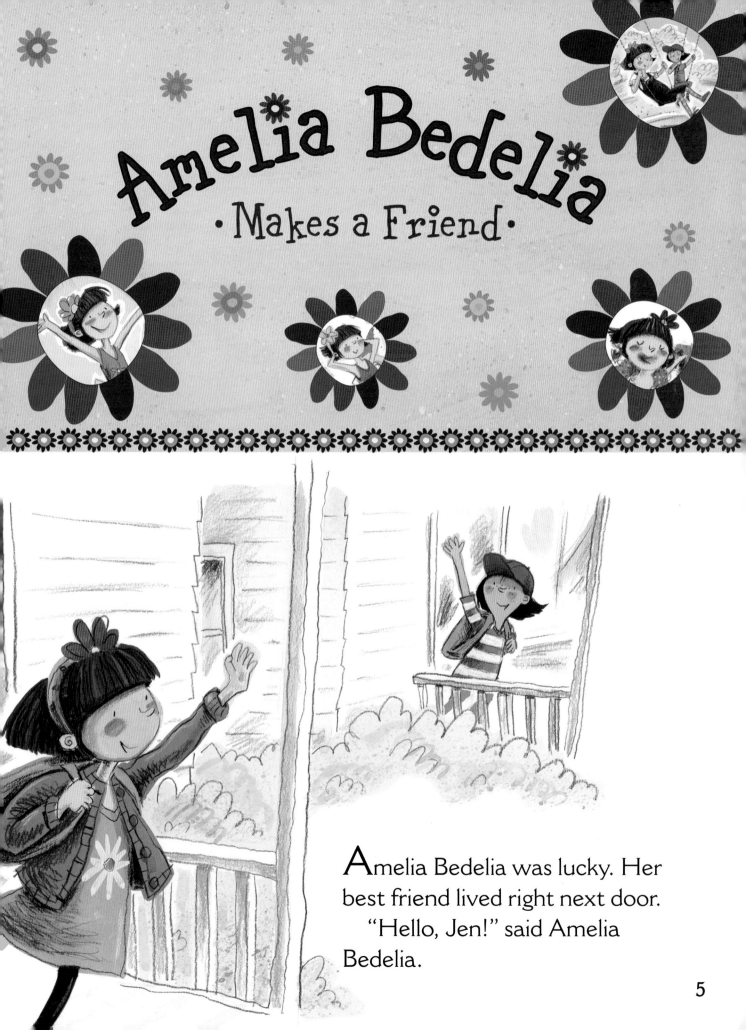

Amelia Bedelia was lucky. Her best friend lived right next door. "Hello, Jen!" said Amelia Bedelia.

"Hi, Amelia Bedelia!" said Jen. Amelia Bedelia and Jen were used to seeing each other almost every day. Amelia Bedelia and Jen had been friends since they were babies.

They baked together.

They dressed up together.

They played music together.
They went to school together.
They did everything together.

Amelia Bedelia even showed Jen how to bowl.
"It's amazing!" said Amelia Bedelia's mother.
"They play so well together."
"They sure do," said Jen's mother. "Even
though they are as different as night and day."

Then one day, Jen and her parents moved away. Even though Amelia Bedelia knew the day was coming, and even though she knew Jen was moving to a new house in a new town, she was very sad. Her parents were sad, too.

Amelia Bedelia missed Jen. She missed
Jen every day. She missed Jen more than
anything. She wished Jen would come back.

One morning, a moving van pulled up to Jen's old house.

Amelia Bedelia and her mother rushed outside.

"Did Jen come back?" asked Amelia Bedelia.

"I don't think so," said Amelia Bedelia's mother. "We must have new neighbors."

While Amelia Bedelia's mother worked in the kitchen, Amelia Bedelia sat at the table and drew pictures.

Amelia Bedelia's mother watched the movers through the window as they moved boxes and furniture into Jen's old house.

"Oh, look," she said. "I see a fancy footstool."

Amelia Bedelia did not look. She just wanted Jen back.

"Look!" said Amelia Bedelia's mother. "I see a coffee table."

Amelia Bedelia still did not look. She just kept drawing.

Amelia Bedelia's mother said, "I see some big armchairs."

A few minutes later she said, "I see a loveseat."

Amelia Bedelia kept right on drawing.

"I see a twin bed," said her mother.

Finally, Amelia Bedelia looked at Jen's house. She couldn't help herself!

Then she looked at her drawings.

"Our new neighbors sound strange," she said.

That night, Amelia Bedelia told her dad about the new neighbors. She showed him her drawings.

He absolutely loved them!

"Amazing!" her dad said with a smile. "I hope they have a pool table."

The next morning, Amelia Bedelia and her mother baked blueberry muffins. Amelia Bedelia loved to bake, especially with her mother.

The muffins looked delicious. Amelia Bedelia and her mother put the muffins in a pretty basket and took them next door.

A lady opened the door. "Hello there," she said. "My name is Mrs. Adams. You must be my new neighbors."

"No," said Amelia Bedelia. "We already live here. We live over there, in our house. You are my new neighbor."

"You know," said Mrs. Adams, "I think both of us are right. How wonderful! Do come in."

"Mmmm," Mrs. Adams said. "What smells so good?"

"My mom does," said Amelia Bedelia. "I don't wear perfume yet."

Amelia Bedelia looked around. Jen's house looked so different. It was not at all like she remembered it. Every room was full of boxes.

"Welcome to my mess," said Mrs. Adams. "I'll be living out of boxes for a while."

That sounded fun to Amelia Bedelia. She would love to live in a box.

"Are the twins already in their bed?" asked Amelia Bedelia.

"My goodness," said Mrs. Adams. "You certainly have sharp eyes."

Amelia Bedelia hoped that was good, even though it sounded a little dangerous.

"My twin grandchildren will visit today," said Mrs. Adams. "And I can't wait! Their names are Mary and Marty."

When the twins visited that afternoon, Mrs. Adams introduced them to Amelia Bedelia.

"Our grandma is lots of fun," they told Amelia Bedelia.

They were right! It was great to have a friend right next door again.

Amelia Bedelia and Mrs. Adams baked together.

They dressed up together.

They played music together. They did all kinds of fantastic things together!

"They have so much fun together," said Amelia
Bedelia's father.

"They sure do," said Amelia Bedelia's mother.
"Even though they are as different as night and day."

One day Jen came back to visit. Amelia Bedelia
was so happy to see her again!

Mrs. Adams took both girls to a real bowling alley.

"This is the best day ever," said Amelia Bedelia. "I
have a best old friend and a best new friend. We are
three best friends together!"

Amelia Bedelia
·Sleeps Over·

Amelia Bedelia was so excited. Tonight was her very first sleepover. All the girls in her class were going to Rose's house for a slumber party.

Amelia Bedelia packed her backpack with everything she thought she might need, and then Amelia Bedelia and her mother drove to Rose's house.

"Is a slumber party fun?" asked Amelia Bedelia. "Because sleeping is boring."

"You might not sleep much," said her mother. "You'll probably play, eat pizza, paint nails . . ."

"Do we paint the nails and then hammer them?" asked Amelia Bedelia. "Or do we hammer them first?"

Amelia Bedelia's mother laughed.

"You'll have fun, sweetie," she said. "I promise."

When Amelia Bedelia arrived at Rose's house, the front door swung open. Her friends ran out to greet her.

Rose's mother came outside, too, to chat with Amelia
Bedelia's mother.

"Good luck," said Amelia Bedelia's mom.

"I think I'll need it!" said Rose's mother. "I am a
light sleeper."

"Me too," said Amelia Bedelia. She reached
into her backpack and pulled out her flashlight.
"I sleep with this light every night."

Amelia Bedelia's mother
kissed Amelia Bedelia.

"Good night, sweetie!" she
said. "Have fun!"

Then the party got started.

The girls went inside and played board games.

Amelia Bedelia had worried that she would be bored, but she wasn't.

Next, everyone went outside and played tag in the yard until the sun began to set.

"The pizza is here!" called Rose's father. "Come and get it!"

"And for dessert," said Rose's mother, "we will toast marshmallows and make s'mores."

"Won't that wreck your toaster?" asked Amelia Bedelia. "Marshmallows melt into gooey, blobby . . ."

Amelia Bedelia could imagine the mess. It would be huge!

Rose's father laughed. "We'll toast them on the grill," he said.

"Oh!" said Amelia Bedelia, relieved.

After the pizza was gone, Dawn speared a marshmallow on Amelia Bedelia's stick.

Holly showed her how to turn it carefully and slowly over the grill to get a crunchy brown skin.

Amelia Bedelia put her marshmallow on top of a chocolate bar between two graham crackers.

"Yum!" said Amelia Bedelia. "I'd like some more, please!"

"Now you know why they're called s'mores!" said Rose.

After many more s'mores, the girls went inside the house.

They put on their pajamas, but it was not time to slumber yet.

Rose's family room was warm and cozy. Amelia Bedelia was excited to be together with her friends at night.

Rose brought out bottles of glittery nail polish in more colors than the rainbow. Every color had the perfect name.

Heather painted Amelia Bedelia's nails with "Shamrock Green" on her left hand, "Blue Iceberg" on her right hand, and "Banana Sunrise" on her right foot. She saved her left foot for "Cotton Candy Cupcake."

Amelia Bedelia sighed and said, "I'm so happy we don't have to hammer them!"

Too soon, the clock struck ten.

"Bedtime, girls!" said Rose's mother. "Lights out, and no giggling allowed!"

Oh well, thought Amelia Bedelia. Here comes the slumber part of this slumber party.

Off went the lights and lamps. On went Amelia Bedelia's flashlight. She showed her friends how to make shadow puppets on the wall.

One by one, the girls fell asleep.

All except Amelia Bedelia. She was not one bit sleepy. She made a rabbit on the wall. Then a barking dog. Then an elephant with a trunk to grab . . .

Oops! Her flashlight went out. "Oh, no," said Amelia Bedelia.

It was strange to be away from home in the dark. What light would keep her company now?

Amelia Bedelia noticed a very bright light peeking into the family room. She pulled back the curtains.

A full moon shone down on her. It was beautiful! But now there was too much light!

Amelia Bedelia dragged her sleeping bag under Rose's Ping-Pong table. Perfect, thought Amelia Bedelia. Now I am having a sleepover and a sleep under.

Amelia Bedelia snuggled down into her cozy sleeping bag. She gazed up at the moon. She had heard people say that there was a man in the moon. She'd never seen him, until tonight. He looked just like her dad.

Amelia Bedelia closed her eyes. A second later, she was sound asleep.

The next morning, the girls had a pillow fight.
Pillow feathers flew everywhere!

Then they made delicious chocolate chip
pancakes and helped to clean up the mess.

Amelia Bedelia's dad picked her up.

"Nice nails," said her father.

"Thanks, moon man," said Amelia Bedelia with a yawn.

"Huh?" said her father. "You sound like you need to take a nap."

And so Amelia Bedelia did, all the way home.

Amelia Bedelia
· Hits the Trail ·

Amelia Bedelia was going hiking. Her entire class was going, too. "Let's hit the trail," said Miss Edwards, Amelia Bedelia's teacher.

The group set out. It was a beautiful day, and soon their school was just a speck in the distance. The trail was steep. Everyone stepped over a big tree root.

Amelia Bedelia was chatting and looking up at the birds and . . . oops! Amelia Bedelia fell flat on her face. Splat!

"Are you okay?" asked Miss Edwards.

"I'm okay," said Amelia Bedelia, brushing herself off. "But the next time I hit the trail, I'll use this stick instead of my face!"

Amelia Bedelia and her friends spotted lots of interesting living things along the trail. They saw a deer and a rabbit. They saw squirrels and chipmunks. They saw insects crawling along the ground and flying in the air. Birds chirped in the trees.

When a snake slithered out of the grass and crossed the trail, Chip let out a yell.

"Relax," said Penny. "That snake is more scared of you than you are of it."

The class walked slowly. There was so much to see and explore, and they didn't want to miss anything!

"Let's move a little faster," said Miss Edwards. "Pick up your snail's pace."

Amelia Bedelia looked for a snail with a pace to pick up. She hunted in the leaves and under bushes and rocks. Maybe she could find one for the classroom nature table.

"I'm hungry," said Clay. "Can we eat lunch now?"

Miss Edwards read her trail map. "Look! There's a stream ahead," she said. "We can stop there for a bite."

"I have lots of bites," said Amelia Bedelia. Amelia Bedelia had noticed that the bugs certainly seemed to like her! She was itching all over.

"I can see water!" said Penny.
The class raced to the stream.
"We'll eat lunch on the bank. Find
a spot and dig in!" said Miss Edwards.

Amelia Bedelia didn't see a bank, or even a cash machine.

Was there treasure buried here?

Why else would Miss Edwards tell them to dig in?

Everyone unpacked their picnics and enjoyed their food in the sun. A gentle breeze made the flowers dance on their stems. The class listened to the birds and the water gently flowing by the bank.

Finally, it was time to go back to school.

Wade was the last to finish his lunch.

"Let's go, Wade," said Miss Edwards, impatiently.

"Yay!" said Amelia Bedelia.

Amelia Bedelia took off her shoes and socks and waded right into the stream.

Soon everyone was splashing with Amelia Bedelia. Even Miss Edwards joined the fun.

As they walked back down the trail, everyone found things for the nature table.

Daisy picked a daisy. Holly plucked a sprig of holly. Rose found a wild rose. Amelia Bedelia picked up fallen leaves.

"What did you find, Amelia Bedelia?" asked Miss Edwards.

"These are my leafs," said Amelia Bedelia.

Miss Edwards smiled. "When you have more than one leaf, you say *leaves*," she said.

That made sense to Amelia Bedelia.

In the fall, every leaf had to leave its tree. It was how the trees got ready for winter.

Amelia Bedelia knew that from now on, she wouldn't think of a leaf falling off a tree. She would think it was leaving its tree. That made much more sense.

"Nice leaves," said Skip when he saw the bunch Amelia Bedelia was carrying. "You have maple, oak, and chestnut."

Skip knew a lot about trees.

"What is this red one?" asked Amelia Bedelia.

"Uh-oh," said Skip. "Look out! That is poison ivy!"

YEE-AHHHH!!

"Yee-AHHHH!" shouted Amelia Bedelia.

Amelia Bedelia threw the leaves up in the air. Her leaves were leaving again!

Skip laughed so hard he fell on the ground.

"I was joking!" he said. He grabbed his stomach and rolled around.

Amelia Bedelia was not laughing. She didn't think Skip's joke was funny at all.

"That was a mean trick," she said.

"Maybe you should take a hike," said Skip.

"I am," said Amelia Bedelia. "And now, thanks to you, I don't have anything for the nature table."

Amelia Bedelia's lip trembled.

"I'm sorry, Amelia Bedelia," said Skip.

He helped Amelia Bedelia pick up her leaves.

"Hold still!" Skip said. He was looking at her back with a surprised expression on his face.

"Are you teasing again?" asked Amelia Bedelia.

"No. You have a hitchhiker," said Skip. He pointed at a caterpillar. The caterpillar was crawling on Amelia Bedelia's backpack.

"Wow!" said Amelia Bedelia.

When the class returned to school, Miss Edwards set up the nature table in their classroom. They displayed flowers and pine cones and sticks and rocks and feathers and acorns—everything they had collected on their hike.

But Amelia Bedelia's caterpillar was the star of the nature table.

Then it was the star of Amelia Bedelia's
classroom . . . until it hit the trail.

Amelia Bedelia
·Tries Her Luck·

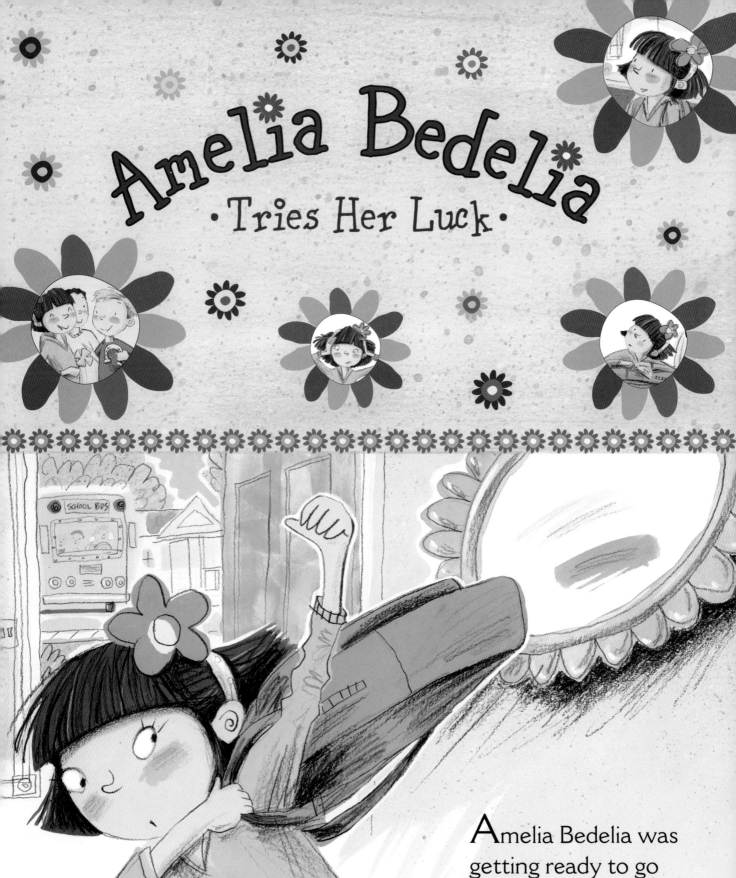

Amelia Bedelia was getting ready to go to school when . . . CRASH!

She bumped into the mirror by the front door
and it broke into pieces!

"I'm sorry!" said Amelia Bedelia.

"Accidents happen, sweetie," said her mother.
"The important thing is that you are not hurt."

At school, Amelia Bedelia told her friends about the accident.

"You're in big trouble," said Clay. "Breaking a mirror means seven years of bad luck."

"Seven years!" said Amelia Bedelia. She couldn't believe it! "That's almost my whole life!"

"It is probably even worse than that," said Rose. "Today is Friday the thirteenth. Bad luck gets doubled today."

"That's fourteen years!" said Amelia Bedelia. "I'll have bad luck forever!"

"Amelia Bedelia," said Joy, "you can change your luck."

"That's right," said Heather. "My dad always says, *See a penny, pick it up, all the day you'll have good luck.*"

Amelia Bedelia picked up her friend Penny.

"Put me down!" said Penny. "Heather means a penny coin, not a Penny person."

At recess, the whole class tried to help Amelia Bedelia change her luck. They hunted everywhere for lucky things. They searched for a four-leaf clover. They looked for a lucky horseshoe. They tried to find a rabbit's foot. Unfortunately, the playground didn't have any of those things.

"I'm sorry, Amelia Bedelia," said Clay. "We struck out. You are out of luck."

When recess was over, Amelia Bedelia got some paper and pencils and drew up a plan. If she could not find luck, she would make her own luck.

Amelia Bedelia's teacher, Miss Edwards, saw her drawings. She also saw that Amelia Bedelia was upset.

"Are you all right?" asked Miss Edwards.

"No, I am all wrong," said Amelia Bedelia. Amelia Bedelia felt as though there was a giant storm cloud of bad luck hanging over her head.

She told Miss Edwards about breaking the mirror before school and her double bad luck.

"Thank you, Amelia Bedelia," said Miss Edwards. "It turns out that today is my lucky day! Friday the thirteenth is the perfect day to talk about luck."

Miss Edwards gathered the class together.

They made a list of lucky and unlucky things on the board. They talked about bad luck and good luck. There were all kinds of questions.

Then Miss Edwards told the class a story.

"When I was your age," she said, "there was one saying that really scared me. It was, *Step on a crack, break your mother's back*."

"That's terrible," said Amelia Bedelia.

"Yes, it is. But it isn't true," said Miss Edwards. "Just like breaking a mirror isn't bad luck."

"Breaking a mirror is bad luck," said Clay. "It's bad luck for the mirror!"

Everyone laughed.

Amelia Bedelia laughed hardest of all. All of a sudden she felt a lot better.

As Amelia Bedelia was walking home from the bus stop, she saw a crack in the sidewalk.

"Bad luck? Ha!" she said.

She stepped on the crack. She stepped on every crack she saw. When she spied the biggest crack of all, Amelia Bedelia jumped up in the air and stomped on it.

Then Amelia Bedelia turned onto her street, and she stopped in her tracks. There was an ambulance in front of her house.

Amelia Bedelia raced home. Breaking the mirror was an accident, but she had stepped on those cracks on purpose. "Mom!" yelled Amelia Bedelia. "I didn't mean to break your back!"

The ambulance was pulling away.

"Mom!" cried Amelia Bedelia. "Mom!"

"Amelia Bedelia!" said her mother. "I'm with Mrs. Adams, sweetie."

Amelia Bedelia whirled around. Her mom was visiting with their neighbor. They were on the porch. Her back was absolutely fine!

Amelia Bedelia ran to her mom and gave her the biggest, longest, strongest hug ever.

"Ouch, honey!" said Amelia Bedelia's mother. "Do you want to break my back?"

"No, never!" said Amelia Bedelia. She hugged her mom again.

"You just missed the excitement," said Mrs. Adams. "You'll never guess what happened! I got a ride home in an ambulance after my checkup."

"Are you okay?" asked Amelia Bedelia.

"I'm fine," said Mrs. Adams. "Knock on wood."

Then Mrs. Adams knocked three times on her porch railing.

Tomorrow, Amelia Bedelia would add "knock on wood" to the list of superstitions her class had made. Today, worrying about luck had worn her out.

Amelia Bedelia thought about her family and how much she loved her mom and dad. She thought about her great friends at school, and how they had helped her feel better. She thought about her old best friend, Jen, and her wonderful new neighbor, Mrs. Adams. She thought that the mirror Mrs. Adams gave her was cool.

Amelia Bedelia felt like she was the luckiest person in the world.

Amelia Bedelia
·Joins the Club·

Amelia Bedelia loved her school. She liked the way everyone got along. They worked together. They played together. They took turns and shared everything.

"Let Pat have a turn."

"Daisy gets the glue next."

"You can go ahead of me."

"I like your idea better."

"This way is easier."

"Try some of my chips."

Amelia Bedelia's class always got
along . . . until it rained. That was
when her class split in two.

"We are the Puddle Stompers!"
said the other half.

Puddle Jumpers took running leaps
and flew over puddles.

Puddle Stompers took running leaps and landed in puddles.

"Come sail over puddles with us," said Clay, as he soared over a big puddle.

"Puddles are not big enough to sail across," said Amelia Bedelia.

"Come dive into puddles with us," said Holly, as she kicked and splashed.

"Puddles are too small to dive into," said Amelia Bedelia.

Both clubs wanted Amelia Bedelia.

Jumping and stomping looked like fun to Amelia Bedelia. She liked every Jumper and Stomper. They were all her friends!

But if she picked one club she might hurt the feelings of her friends in the other club.

Amelia Bedelia asked Miss Edwards, her teacher, for help.

"It sounds like you are torn between two choices," said Miss Edwards.

"You're right," said Amelia Bedelia. "I am torn. And it really hurts!"

After school, when everyone was waiting for the buses, the Stompers and the Jumpers tried to make Amelia Bedelia choose one club or the other.

"I'll decide at recess tomorrow," Amelia Bedelia told them, as she got on her bus to head home.

Amelia Bedelia's mother was waiting for her at the bus stop.

"Rain, rain, go away. Come again another day!" said her mother.

"Oh, Mom, not another day," said Amelia Bedelia. "How about never! Rain and puddles, don't come here. Come again another year!"

"Sorry, sweetie," said her mother, popping open her umbrella. "It is going to rain buckets tonight."

Amelia Bedelia was worried. Buckets of rain tonight meant millions of puddles tomorrow!

At supper, Amelia Bedelia told her parents about the Jumpers and the Stompers and about being caught between the two clubs.

"Wow!" said her father. "You are in a club sandwich."

Amelia Bedelia knew her dad was joking, but at least he knew how she felt.

"Why choose?" asked her mother. "Can't you join two clubs?"

Amelia Bedelia stopped chewing. That was the answer!

She hugged her mom.

At last Amelia Bedelia knew just what to do.

The next day, it stopped raining right before recess.

The playground was filled with oodles of puddles. There were big ones and deep ones and small ones and muddy ones.

The Jumpers and the Stompers rushed outside.

Everyone was excited. Everyone wanted to hear which club Amelia Bedelia was going to join.

"I am joining my own club!" said Amelia Bedelia. "It is called the Hop, Skip, and Jump club."

Then she showed them what she did in her club.

First Amelia Bedelia hopped over a puddle.

"Hooray!" said the Jumpers.

Then Amelia Bedelia skipped to another puddle and jumped into it with a splash.

"Yippee!" cried the Stompers.

Every one of the Jumpers and Stompers wanted to be in the Hop, Skip, and Jump club. Even Miss Edwards!

"Nice work, Amelia Bedelia," said Miss Edwards. "By joining your own club, you joined the other two clubs together."

Amelia Bedelia was not thinking about
that. She was just happy to see her class
getting along again, even in the rain.

Amelia Bedelia
·Chalks One Up·

Amelia Bedelia and her mother looked out the window. Amelia Bedelia's mother was as glum as the weather.

"Where is the sun?" she asked. "I am really blue."

Amelia Bedelia looked at her mother. She was not blue. She was not even wearing anything blue.

She was not wearing a smile, either.

Amelia Bedelia's friend Rose was coming over, and that gave Amelia Bedelia an idea.

"I am having a playdate, Mom," she said. "Maybe you should have one, too."

"Great idea, sweetie!" said Amelia Bedelia's mom.

She made two short phone calls, one to Amelia Bedelia's dad and one to their neighbor Mrs. Adams.

Then she said, "I am going to town. After I go shopping, I'll meet Dad for coffee. Mrs. Adams will watch you and Rose. She's waiting for us now."

Mrs. Adams was right outside.

"Have fun," she said to Amelia Bedelia's mother. "And don't worry about us girls. We'll have a ball."

Amelia Bedelia's mother waved goodbye. "Well, chalk up another gray day!" she said. "And thank you for your good idea, sweetie!"

As Amelia Bedelia waved back, she got an even better idea.

Amelia Bedelia found her big bucket of chalk in the garage.

When Rose's father dropped Rose off, Amelia Bedelia was already hard at work.

"Wow!" said Rose. "You have every color in the rainbow!"

"I need them," said Amelia Bedelia. "I'm chalking up a gray day to make my mom happy. Want to help?"

"Sure!" said Rose.

To warm up their drawing arms, Amelia Bedelia and Rose drew squares for hopscotch on the sidewalk in front of Amelia Bedelia's house.

When they played a game, Mrs. Adams was amazing!

Just then, Amelia Bedelia's friend Chip walked by
with his big brother and their puppy, Scout.
   "Hey, what's going on?" yelled Chip.
   "We're chalking up a gray day," said Amelia Bedelia.
"Want to help?"
   "Cool!" said Chip.

"What makes your mom really happy, Amelia Bedelia?" asked Rose.

"She likes flowers and green and growing things," said Amelia Bedelia, pointing to where plants grew last year.

Rose got green, red, and pink chalk from the bucket. She began drawing roses on Amelia Bedelia's house.

"Hey, Amelia Bedelia!"

Daisy was walking by with her babysitter and her new baby sister. "What are you doing?" she asked.

"Chalking up a gray day," said Amelia Bedelia. "Want to help?"

"Yes!" said Daisy.

Daisy began drawing daisies, using different colors.

"That's my mom's favorite flower," said Amelia Bedelia. "She'll love those. Thanks!"

Amelia Bedelia told her friends about her mom's favorite spots in town. Amelia Bedelia's mom loved the library and a flower store called Blooms, and lots of other places.

Chip drew a map. Amelia Bedelia, Rose, and Daisy added shops and places to eat.

While Amelia Bedelia and her friends were working, Mrs. Adams made tasty treats for everyone.

"What great drawings," she said, when she came back outside. "Roll out the red carpet for your mom!"

Amelia Bedelia didn't have one. So they drew a carpet with red chalk, leading to the best surprise of all.

Then Amelia Bedelia saw their car pulling into the driveway.

Her parents had come home together.

"Hi, Mom!" said Amelia Bedelia. "Welcome back!"

"You guys really went to town," said Amelia Bedelia's father. He took out his phone and snapped some pictures.

"Not us," said Amelia Bedelia. "Mom went to town. We stayed home and drew!"

Amelia Bedelia's parents followed the red carpet across the driveway and to the backyard.

Everyone else followed them. They all stopped in front of an amazing mural on the side of the garage.

"A yellow sun plus a blue mom makes green," said Amelia Bedelia. "And green makes you happy!"

Amelia Bedelia's mother was speechless.
She hugged each of them. And she hugged
Amelia Bedelia the longest of all.
Amelia Bedelia's dad took more photographs.

It was a good thing he did. It rained all night long. The chalk washed away, and the pictures melted. All the colors of the rainbow soaked into the earth.

The next day was bright and sunny. Amelia Bedelia and her mom stood at the window feeling yellow and pink and green and every other color . . . except blue.

Amelia Bedelia
·Is for the Birds·

Amelia Bedelia loved her swing set. She had loved it when she was a baby and she still loved it now that she was big.

Every day when Amelia Bedelia got home from school, she raced outside and hopped on her swing. She swung back and forth fifty times. Higher and higher and higher until she was practically flying.

Then she slid down the slide five times. Wheee!!!!!

After that she ran inside for a snack and did her homework.

This was Amelia Bedelia's routine, and it made her happy.

Pendulums

One afternoon, Amelia Bedelia found a messy pile of sticks and leaves and grass on the top of her slide.

"Yuck!" she said, as she swept everything onto the ground. "Who made this mess on my slide?"

She slid down the slide superfast and raced across the yard.

Some birds began chirping loudly and fluttering around her head. They were not singing a happy song.

Amelia Bedelia had a feeling the birds were mad at her. She couldn't remember birds acting quite like that before!

Amelia Bedelia ran into the kitchen.

"Look, Mom," she said, pointing out the window. "I think those birds made a mess on my slide, and they've been squawking at me."

They watched the birds pile more twigs and leaves and grass on the top of the slide. The birds seemed to be working together.

"Oh, how sweet," said Amelia Bedelia's mother. "The robins are building a nest on your slide."

"But they can't do that," said Amelia Bedelia. "I use my slide every day. It's my routine!"

"Well, I guess you could scare them away," said her mother. "Or you could let them build a nest and start a family."

"You mean there will be baby birds?" asked Amelia Bedelia. "Born in our backyard, on my slide?"

She gobbled down her snack.

"I'm going to my swing set, Mom!" she said.

"Halt, young lady," said her mother, pointing at Amelia Bedelia's books. "Your homework comes first."

After homework, dinner, and the dishes, Amelia Bedelia finally went back outside. Luckily, the sun hadn't set quite yet.

She felt really bad about wrecking the bird nest. She gathered more twigs and leaves and grass to replace what she had tossed away. She raced to her room and got yarn, scraps of felt, and fluffy feathers from her arts-and-crafts box. She left neat little heaps of stuff at the bottom of her slide.

"Here you go, Mr. and Mrs. Robin!" she called to the birds. "This is a nest supply shop just for you! I'm sorry I wrecked your home before."

The next day Amelia Bedelia woke up early.

Birds were chirping and singing right outside her window. They had been up for hours, working away.

Amelia Bedelia was amazed. The birds had been very busy.

"Wow!" said Amelia Bedelia at breakfast. "Look at their new nest!"

"It reminds me of one of your art projects, sweetie," said her mother, smiling.

"Try these binoculars," said her father. "They will make your bird's-eye view even better."

Amelia Bedelia looked through her dad's binoculars. She watched the birds before school and after school and as often as possible.

The mother robin sat on the nest day and night, in rain and shine. She sat there for almost two weeks.

One day Amelia Bedelia saw something new.

"Look, Mom!" she said. "There are four tiny blue eggs!"

"How sweet," said her mother. "They are robin's-egg blue."

"Of course they are," said Amelia Bedelia. "What other color would they be?"

Finally, one day after school Amelia Bedelia spotted the mother bird on the top of the slide holding a worm in her beak.

Her babies were peeping. "Feed me, feed me, feed me, feed me!"

The eggs had hatched. There were four baby robins snuggling in the nest.

At dinner that night Amelia Bedelia's father talked about a mess he had fixed at his job. "The situation was a real can of worms," he said. "But I think I cleaned it up."

"Hey, Dad," said Amelia Bedelia. "The next time someone at work opens a can of worms, bring some home for our robins."

The robin family gave Amelia Bedelia a new routine. She watched them every morning before school and every afternoon when she got home.

She saw the baby birds get bigger. She watched their feathers grow. She saw them leave the nest for the first time.

One day she watched them fly away. Amelia Bedelia was so sad! It was like saying goodbye to best friends!

"When you grow up, you'll spread your wings and fly away, too," said her father. "We'll have an empty nest, just like Mr. and Mrs. Robin."

Amelia Bedelia did not believe it, but she knew it might be true.

Now Amelia Bedelia's mom's eyes were all watery, the way they were when she watched her favorite movies.

"That's a long way off, sweetie," her mom said.

Amelia Bedelia waited a few days to make sure the robins were really gone. Then she climbed up her slide and carefully took the nest down.

Amelia Bedelia brought the nest to school to show her class. She told them about the robin family.

"That's amazing!" said Miss Edwards, Amelia Bedelia's teacher. "How did you find out so much about robins?"

"A little birdie told me," said Amelia Bedelia.

Amelia Bedelia
·By the Yard·

GARAGE SALE

One day Amelia Bedelia and her parents were coming home from the park. They drove by a sign poking out of the grass.

Amelia Bedelia's mother shouted, "Pull over, pull over!"

Amelia Bedelia looked out her window. She did not see a pullover sweater. She did see lots of stuff for sale, though.

All the stuff was spread out in someone's front yard.

Amelia Bedelia's mother jumped out of the car. "I'll be right back," she said.

"Mom loves garage sales," said Amelia Bedelia's father.

"Is she buying a new garage?" asked Amelia Bedelia.
Amelia Bedelia's father shook his head. "No, but we
could use another garage just to hold all the stuff she
buys at garage sales," he said.

A few minutes later Amelia Bedelia's mother brought back two treasures.

She handed a big book of stories to Amelia Bedelia.

She tossed a purple sweater to Amelia Bedelia's father. "It's a pullover," she said. "Try it on!"

"Is that the one you saw from the car?" said Amelia Bedelia.

Amelia Bedelia's father had already pulled the sweater over his head.

"Did you hear about the big garage sale next Saturday?" he said.

"Where?" asked Amelia Bedelia's mother. Her eyes lit up.

"At our house," he said. "Let's get rid of our clutter. We need to weed out!"

For the next week, Amelia Bedelia and her parents sorted through the things they had not used in years.

They checked their closets and drawers and shelves and cabinets and even under their beds.

By Saturday, they were ready for their very own garage sale—except for one thing.

Amelia Bedelia was not happy about their sign, which said GARAGE SALE.

"You can't sell our garage," said Amelia Bedelia. "Where will our car sleep? Plus, the garage matches our house."

"Oh, honey," said Amelia Bedelia's mother. "We'd never sell the garage!"

"Let's try a different idea," said Amelia Bedelia's father.

He held up a new sign. It said YARD SALE.

"Is this better?"

"No!" wailed Amelia Bedelia. "That's worse. I love our yard even more than our garage."

"Okay. We won't sell either one," said Amelia Bedelia's mother. "We will just sell the things we put in the yard."

People began stopping to look.
It got crowded fast. There were
cars parked up and down the street.

Amelia Bedelia's
parents were busy.

Amelia Bedelia helped, too.

"Nice sewing machine," said a woman. "It's just what I'm looking for. Can you throw in a yardstick?"

"Sure," said Amelia Bedelia. "I'll be right back."

She ran behind the garage. There was a big pile of leaves and sticks there. She got as many sticks as she could carry.

"Here you go," said Amelia Bedelia. "These sticks are from our yard. Pick one. I'll throw it in."

The lady laughed.

"I am looking for a yardstick that is thirty-six inches long," she said.

Amelia Bedelia grabbed a tall ruler from a messy box of stuff. She used it to measure the longest stick. "This one is exactly thirty-six inches!" she said.

"Perfect," said the woman. "If I buy the sewing machine, and take the stick, will you throw in that ruler, too?"

"I'll hand it to you," said Amelia Bedelia.

"It's a deal," said the woman.

She looked around the yard.

"I'm making curtains," she said. "I'll need yards of fabric. Do you think you can help me find that?"

"Yards?" said Amelia Bedelia. "That's a lot of fabric. That would cover up my mom's flowers."

"The flowers are absolutely beautiful," said the woman. "I would love to buy some of your mother's plants."

"You can," said Amelia Bedelia. "My dad says we are weeding out. Everything in the yard is for sale."

Amelia Bedelia found a shovel. She dug up some plants for the woman.

By the end of the day, everything was sold.

Amelia Bedelia's parents were shocked to see the big holes in their yard.

"Amazing," said Amelia Bedelia's father. "At our yard sale, even the yard got sold."

Amelia Bedelia's mother sighed. "Who would buy the yard?" she asked.

"A nice lady," said Amelia Bedelia. "I helped her as much as I could. She does everything by the yard."

"Well," said Amelia Bedelia's mother. "My plants will grow back soon. I do like getting rid of clutter. It's relaxing, and it makes things easier to find."

"The only thing I want to find is a pizza," said Amelia Bedelia's father.

On the way to the pizza place, they passed another sign. GARAGE SALE TOMORROW, it said. Amelia Bedelia held her breath.

And this time, Amelia Bedelia's mother did not say a single word.

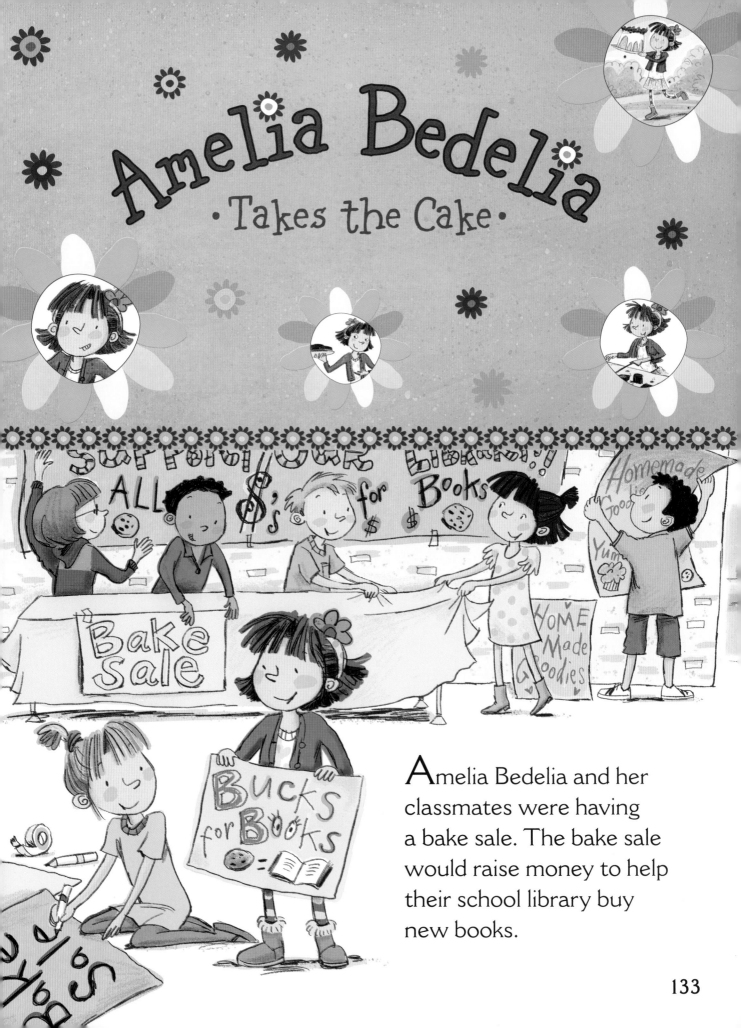

Amelia Bedelia
·Takes the Cake·

Amelia Bedelia and her classmates were having a bake sale. The bake sale would raise money to help their school library buy new books.

Angel arrived with a beautiful cake. "My mom helped me make an angel food cake," said Angel.

Amelia Bedelia thought everything Angel ate was angel food.

Chip came to school carrying a plate of yummy brownies. "I made chocolate chip brownies," said Chip.

"Of course," said Amelia Bedelia.

Amelia Bedelia was excited to share the super chewy brownies she had made.

Just then, Wade arrived with brownies. So did Dawn and Holly and Heather. Teddy and Clay brought brownies, too. So did the rest of the class. There were a lot of brownies!

"People," said Chip. "This is a bake sale, not a brownie festival."

Miss Edwards, their teacher, arrived with a big glass jar to hold the money from the sale.

"My goodness," she said, looking at the brownies. "I've seen lots of mix-ups, but this takes the cake."

"Please do not take our cake!" said Amelia Bedelia. "It's the only one we've got."

Amelia Bedelia didn't want to lose Angel's angel food cake!

"Don't worry, Amelia Bedelia. I'll buy the cake," said Miss Edwards. "I have plans for it!"

"Thank you," said Angel. "I hope you like it." She put the money from Miss Edwards in the big glass jar.

"Go ahead and get set up," said Miss Edwards. "I'll be right back."

Amelia Bedelia and her classmates stared at stacks of brownies.

"Maybe we should just put out a few at a time," said Dawn.

Clay and Teddy gave her idea a try. They put out six brownies in a neat line.

"That looks weird," said Wade. "We did a lot of baking, but I do not think we will sell a lot that way."

"I know," said Amelia Bedelia. "Let's put them all out at once!"

The brownies were all square. They were all about the same size. But the light, cakey ones were tall.

The dark, chewy ones were short. Some had flaky tops. Others were smooth and flat. Teddy had put icing on his batch.

Holly had dusted her batch
with powdered sugar.

The bakers stood back to admire their work.
"That looks amazing," said Penny. "I've never
seen so much chocolate."
"It's cool," said Skip. "They are the same but
also not the same."

Cliff squinted his eyes.

"Too bad we can't make one big brownie!" he said. "We could set a world record for biggest brownie."

Amelia Bedelia squinted her eyes. She could see what Cliff saw. She also saw something else. She began moving brownies here and there and everywhere while her classmates watched.

Finally, Amelia Bedelia stood back to admire her work. "Now that is one big brown 'E'!" she said.

141

Everyone laughed and cheered.
"That is amazing," said Angel.
"That's great, Amelia Bedelia," said Clay.
"But we definitely need new signs."

Everyone got right to work.

Soon, kids from other classes came to the bake sale. Parents and babysitters stopped by. So did teachers and bus drivers. The principal and the school nurse visited, too. Everyone wanted a taste of the biggest brown "E" in town. Soon they were completely sold out!

"Wow!" said Miss Edwards when she returned. "I've
been to many bake sales, but this one really does take
the cake!"

"No, you bought the cake!" said Amelia Bedelia.

"You're right! I did," said Miss Edwards. "I thought
the best bakers in town might like a delicious snack
when their work was done."

"Thanks, Miss Edwards," said Angel. She was trying to smile but she couldn't help feeling disappointed. "I do like angel food cakes, but I really wanted to try a brownie. We sold out before I got a taste."

"Well, sometimes you can't have your cake and eat it, too," said Miss Edwards. "The great thing is that you raised a lot of money for the library."

"What good is having a cake if you can't eat it?" asked Amelia Bedelia.

"Good point," said Miss Edwards. She cut the cake into even slices. There was enough for everyone.

Amelia Bedelia and her classmates enjoyed the treat.

"This cake is really good, Angel!" said Amelia Bedelia. "Thanks for baking it."

This time, they could have their cake and eat it, too!

Amelia Bedelia
·On the Move·

Amelia Bedelia loved to ride around town in the car with her parents. It was fun to wonder what was inside other people's houses.

"Where are we going today?" asked Amelia Bedelia.

"We are house hunting," said Amelia Bedelia's father.

Amelia Bedelia looked out her window.

"The houses are not hiding," she said. "I see one, two, three, four. Hunting for houses is easy."

"We are looking for houses that are for sale," said Amelia Bedelia's mother. "Look at that pretty Tudor house!"

"Our house has two doors," said Amelia Bedelia.

"Wait a minute," said her father. "Don't we have a front door, a back door, and a garage door?"

"That's right," said Amelia Bedelia. "We live in a three-door house."

"A Tudor-style house looks like an English home in the Middle Ages," explained Amelia Bedelia's mother. "Tudor-style homes are easy to spot."

"Did you know that there were many kings and queens in the Tudor family?" asked her father. "King Henry was a famous Tudor king," her mother added.

"Let's look for a colonial house," said Amelia Bedelia's father.

"Colonial-style homes have been popular since the American Revolution," said Amelia Bedelia's mother.

"How many colonies were there in 1776?" asked Amelia Bedelia's father.

"Thirteen!" shouted Amelia Bedelia from the backseat.

"Hey look!" said Amelia Bedelia's mother. "That ranch is having an open house."

"Let's go in," said her father.

"Hooray!" said Amelia Bedelia. "I love horses."

During the holidays, Amelia Bedelia's parents always had an open-house party. Friends and neighbors were free to stop by anytime.

It didn't look as though there was a party at the ranch, though. The house was quiet.

"Are we the first ones?" asked Amelia Bedelia.

The front door swung wide open.

"Welcome home!" said a smiling woman with a name tag that read JILL.

"Oh, I don't live here," said Amelia Bedelia. "I live at my house. We came to look at your ranch."

"Well, come right in," said Jill.

Homes by Jill

Hi, I'm Jill, your real estate agent.
Let me find the perfect home
for you!!!

Style: Ranch
Built: 1952
Square Feet: 2,500

Bedrooms: 3
Bathrooms: 1.5
Hardwood floors and full,
finished basement.
Acres: 1

Jill gave Amelia Bedelia a piece of paper. "Here are some facts about the house," she said. "But I'm not the owner. I'm an agent."

Amelia Bedelia whispered in her mother's ear.

Her mother smiled and said, "No, sweetie, Jill is not a spy. Not all agents are secret agents. Jill is a real estate agent."

"Let me show you around," said Jill. "What are you looking for?"

"Well, we're running out of room," said Amelia Bedelia's mother.

"We need about six hundred more square feet," said her father. "At least."

Amelia Bedelia knew her father had two flat feet. Why did he want so many square ones?

$8ft \times 10ft = 80 sq ft$

8'

BEDROOM

10'

$2 \times 300 sq' = 600 sq'$

"Let's go upstairs," said Amelia Bedelia. "I want to pick out my bedroom."

"A ranch-style house does not have an upstairs," said her father. "A ranch house is built like a house on a ranch out west."

"So where do we sleep?" asked Amelia Bedelia.

"On this floor," said her mother.

Amelia Bedelia stretched out on the floor and imagined sleeping there.

"This house has hardwood floors," said Jill.

"It sure does!" said Amelia Bedelia. "This floor is really hard."

Amelia Bedelia had an idea. While her parents toured the house, she would hunt for the horses. Horses were the best thing about a ranch!

"Where is the backyard?" asked Amelia Bedelia.

"Go through the mudroom," said Jill, pointing to a door, "and you'll see it."

There wasn't any mud in the mudroom—just places to store coats and boots.

Amelia Bedelia opened the back door. She could see the Tudor and the colonial. She could see two dogs and a garden.

Where were the horses hiding?

"Come take a look downstairs," said Jill, when Amelia Bedelia returned to the living room. "This house has a full basement."

"Our basement was full once," said Amelia Bedelia. "It flooded when a pipe broke."

"This basement is finished," said Jill.

"So was ours," said Amelia Bedelia.

"There is a huge rec room," said Jill.

"Our whole basement was wrecked," said Amelia Bedelia.

Amelia Bedelia's parents came downstairs.

"Aha! Here you are," said Amelia Bedelia's father.

"What a great recreation room," said Amelia Bedelia's mother.

"Lots of space for fun and games," said Amelia Bedelia.

After Amelia Bedelia and Jill played a game of Ping-Pong, Jill walked Amelia Bedelia and her parents to the front door.

"Thanks for stopping by," she said. "Now that I know what you want, I'll keep my ear to the ground."

Amelia Bedelia's stomach growled.

Jill must have heard it. Her father did.

"Lunchtime," said Amelia Bedelia's father. "I'm so hungry I could eat a horse."

"Then let's go," said Amelia Bedelia. "You won't find a horse at this ranch."

Amelia Bedelia
•Gets a Break•

Amelia Bedelia was taking care of the class pet over school break.

Amelia Bedelia was so excited. Harry the hamster was actually here in her room!

She moved her dollhouse into her closet to make room for his habitat. Amelia Bedelia loved her dollhouse. She sometimes wished she was small enough to live in it.

That night, Amelia Bedelia snuggled under her covers. She heard Harry squeak as he raced around on his wheel.

"Good night, Harry," said Amelia Bedelia.

She liked having a pet project.

In the morning, Amelia Bedelia let Harry sleep in. She went down to the kitchen and made breakfast for him.

Dawn and Clay stopped by.

"We miss Harry," said Dawn.

"You can help me feed him," said Amelia Bedelia.

Amelia Bedelia took Dawn and Clay up to her room.

"Where is Harry?" asked Dawn.

"Still sleeping," said Amelia Bedelia.

"Are you sure?" said Clay. "His house looks empty to me."

"Oh no, Amelia Bedelia! Harry must have broken out," said Dawn.

"I didn't see a rash," said Amelia Bedelia.

"Harry made a break for it," said Clay.

He looked under Amelia Bedelia's bed. "He escaped. Vanished. Harry is gone," said Dawn.

Amelia Bedelia's lower lip trembled. She wanted to break into tears.

"It is not your fault," said Dawn, hugging Amelia Bedelia.

"Hamsters are brave and curious," said Clay. "Harry is probably exploring."

"When my cat was lost, I made posters. My neighbors saw them and brought her back," said Dawn. "Let's try that!"

Amelia Bedelia got out her art supplies, and the three friends got to work.

165

Soon, Amelia Bedelia felt better. It felt good just to do something. The posters also made her remember Harry's tiny ears and bright eyes. She missed his whiskers most of all.

Harry was an awesome class pet!

"We should really call him Harry Houdini," said Clay.

"Who?" asked Amelia Bedelia.

"Houdini," said Clay.

"He was a famous magician," said Dawn. "He could escape from anyplace. My grandpa told me about him."

"I am learning some magic tricks over the break," said Clay. "My parents signed me up for lessons."

"I know—let's offer a reward," said Dawn.

"Don't count on me," said Clay. "I'm broke."

"You look fine to me," said Amelia Bedelia. "What part of you is broken?"

"I mean, I do not have any money," said Clay.

Clay nibbled a carrot.

"Hey, hands off," said Dawn. "That treat is for Harry."

"I am a magician," said Clay, waving the carrot in the air and then taking a big bite. "I am making this carrot disappear."

"Please make Harry appear," said Amelia Bedelia.

Amelia Bedelia, Dawn, and Clay decided to search for Harry one more time.

"Harry may be gone for good," said Clay, checking under Amelia Bedelia's bed again.

"There is nothing good about that," said Amelia Bedelia.

"He must be close by," said Dawn. "Let's keep looking. We can't give up!"

"Why do you think Harry ran away?" asked Clay. "He has lots of cool stuff in his habitat. I want to run on his wheel, don't you?"

"Do a magic spell and shrink yourself," said Dawn. "Then find Harry."

That is when an idea popped into Amelia Bedelia's head. She tiptoed to her dollhouse. She peeked inside. Sure enough, Harry was asleep on the bed.

Amelia Bedelia felt like cheering. Then she remembered that hamsters stay awake at night and sleep all day. Harry looked so cozy she didn't want to bother him!

"Shhh! Come over here!
Look!" said Amelia Bedelia.

Clay, Dawn, and Amelia
Bedelia watched Harry snooze.
"Who is next to him?" said
Dawn.
Clay was counting. ". . . four,
five, six! I see six babies. Harry
is a father!"

"No. Harry is a mother," said Dawn.
Amelia Bedelia couldn't believe it! There
was a hamster family in her dollhouse!

"Wow! Harry needs a new name," said Amelia Bedelia.
"A new name for a new mom," said Dawn.
They thought and thought and thought.

Bunny Izzy Sweety Cuddles
Penelope Cookie Pixie Fluffernutter
Daisy Violet Poopsie Zizzie
Nibble Dinky Rosie Zoey
Lily Butterscotch Lady Ginger
Ivy Cupcake Tinkerbell Olivia
Squeakie Tilly Honey Goldilocks
Sugar

Clay snapped his fingers. "Presto!" he said. "How about Harriet?"

"Perfect," said Amelia Bedelia.

Amelia Bedelia knew exactly what to do next. They called Miss Edwards. They told their teacher the whole story.

She laughed and laughed.

"Who knew that Harry was really Harriet!" said Amelia Bedelia.

"Sounds like our class pet pulled the wool over our eyes," said Miss Edwards.

"So far, this break has been really fun," said Amelia Bedelia.

"Our class pet got lost, had a family, and got found," said Dawn. "And got a new name!"

"Shazam!" said Clay.

"This has been our lucky break," Amelia Bedelia said to her friends. "We lost one class pet, but we found seven! And we did it all together!"

Amelia Bedelia
·Under the Weather·

Amelia Bedelia did not feel well. She snuggled down in bed with her stuffed animals all around her.

177

The rain and wind hammered on her window. It was a stormy day!

"ROAR! What a zoo!" said Amelia Bedelia's father when he came in to check on her.

"ACHOO!" said Amelia Bedelia.

"Don't tease her, honey. She does not feel well," said Amelia Bedelia's mother.

Amelia Bedelia coughed.

"I am sorry that you are under the weather," said Amelia Bedelia's father.

"I'm not," said Amelia Bedelia, sitting up. "I'm under my covers."

Amelia Bedelia felt dizzy. She fell back on her pillow.

"You are definitely sick," said her mother. "I am calling the school. You're staying home today."

Amelia Bedelia was happy. No school!

Then she was sad. "I'll miss my friends," she said.

"I do not want to rain on your parade," said her mother, "but I've heard that something is going around."

"Not me," said Amelia Bedelia. "I am staying right here."

Before he left for work,
Amelia Bedelia's father carried
Amelia Bedelia downstairs. He
tucked her into his special chair
in front of the TV.

"Thanks, Daddy," said
Amelia Bedelia.
"I'll check on you later,"
he said, blowing her a kiss.

"You may have a fever," said Amelia
Bedelia's mother. "I'll find a thermometer
to take your temperature."
She turned on the TV.

"Not the weather," said Amelia Bedelia. "The weather is boring."

She didn't have the energy to change the channel. She sighed and looked at the storm clouds on the TV screen. "I am under the weather," she said. "And now I am in front of it, too."

Amelia Bedelia did not know why grown-ups worried about the weather. Whether it would rain. Whether it would snow. Whether it would freeze or hail or blow. Amelia Bedelia never worried about it.

She had fun in all kinds of weather. When it snowed, she built forts and snow-people. When it was windy, she flew her kite. When it was hot and sunny, she loved to go the beach. And she loved to eat apples and jump in piles of leaves on crisp, cool days.

Amelia Bedelia's mother returned and put a thermometer under Amelia Bedelia's tongue.

"I will be right back," her mother said.

Amelia Bedelia watched the weather all over the world.

"Ey ook! Eets wane hats een hogs!" said Amelia Bedelia.

Her mother took the thermometer out of Amelia Bedelia's mouth.

"What did you say?" she asked.

"Hey, look! It is raining cats and dogs!" said Amelia Bedelia.

"Poor sweetie," said her mother. "You have a little fever."

The telephone rang. It was Amelia Bedelia's father. Amelia Bedelia's mother handed her the phone.

"Hey, sunshine," he said. "How are you?"

"I am sick," said Amelia Bedelia.

"Are you feeling green around the gills?" her father asked.

Is that how she was feeling, Amelia Bedelia wondered. Like a fish?

Just then there was a knock at the door. Mrs. Adams arrived carrying a big pot. It smelled delicious!

"Yoo-hoo! Howdy, neighbor," said Mrs. Adams. "It is raining buckets out there!"

"And cats and dogs, too," said Amelia Bedelia.

YOO-HOO!

"I hear you are not feeling so hot," said Mrs. Adams.
"I am feeling very hot," said Amelia Bedelia.
"Amelia Bedelia is running a fever," said her mother.
"I am way too sick to run, Mom," said Amelia
Bedelia.

"Well, I have something good for what is making you sick," said Mrs. Adams. "Chicken soup!"

"Thank you," said Amelia Bedelia. "But I need something bad for what is making me sick."

"Oh, dear. Do you have a stomach bug?" asked Mrs. Adams.

"Yuck!" said Amelia Bedelia. "I hope not!"

"You have some kind of bug, sweetie," said Amelia Bedelia's mother.

YUCK!!

"I wish it had wings," said Amelia Bedelia, imagining a huge butterfly soaring over the clouds. "Then I could fly above the weather, instead of being under it."

Later, Amelia Bedelia's father came home.
The weather was still on TV.
"You must be on top of the weather by now," he said.
"It will be partly cloudy tomorrow," said Amelia Bedelia. She had memorized the forecast and knew all the details.
"Not partly sunny?" asked her father.
"Daddy, that is the same thing!" said Amelia Bedelia.
"That sounds more like my daughter," said Amelia Bedelia's father. "You must be feeling better."

"Soon you will be as right as rain," said her mother, serving up a warm bowl of chicken soup. "Come rain or shine!" said Amelia Bedelia.